For RJ and Michael Travis,
my dream catchers.

Prologue

Deep within the Forest of Leeds the adult bears would say that Mr. Biddle is the most polite, intelligent, responsible, and well-dressed bear in all of England. On a perfect day, Mr. Biddle enjoys an English breakfast of smoked trout, fresh seasonal berries, and croissants with butter and black currant jam — ensuring that no savory flavor touches the other.

After breakfast, Mr. Biddle strolls down the path to Twickenham Library, where he spends much of his day reading. His favorite subject is history. There is nothing more exciting to Mr. Biddle than studying ancient tales from the past.

Often in the afternoon, he goes fishing with his best friend, Alexander Tortoise. They discuss important matters such as, "Why are bees so small?" and "Where does snow go when it melts?" In the evenings, Mr. Biddle enjoys spending time inside his cozy home at 858 Bearington Place, which is several miles away from the Town Square.

After a hot supper, Mr. Biddle and Nigel Owl can be found at his desk studying maps and photographs of far away places. He dreams of one day seeing the Australian rain forests and the Great Barrier Reef.

Every now and then, on special days, perhaps twice a year, Mr. Biddle receives a letter from his grandfather, The Great Horatio Biddle. His grandfather is the bravest, wisest, most adventurous, and most respected bear in the world. Mr. Biddle loves reading about his grandfather's travels to dangerous lands and learning how to carry the family name with honor.

Even though Mr. Biddle is studious, thoughtful, and well-dressed, he remains a shy bear. Letters from The Great Horatio Biddle give Mr. Biddle the hope that one day he could be as brave as his grandfather.

*T*wilight melted away. The early morning air was brimming with the sounds of life and cool, gentle breezes.

Nightingales sang from the tree tops and crickets chirped happily in the dew-drenched grasses.

It was the first day of autumn — a time for great celebration throughout the Forest of Leeds.

Nestled in his warm bed, Mr. Biddle was awakening from a long night's sleep.

"Aaahhh!" yawned the bear, stretching himself out.

A few minutes later, he stood up, got dressed, and hummed merrily as he went down the stairs. He was in a very good mood.

The soft silence of the morning was broken by a rumbling sound.

"Why, that's my stomach!" Mr. Biddle thought aloud.

He took a golden watch from his vest pocket, examined it, and said, *"Well now, it's time for a proper breakfast."*

At this moment, he put the watch back into his pocket, opened the front door, and eagerly stepped outside. The sky was a bright, endless blue, and the damp ground glistened as if it were sprinkled with glittering jewels.

"What a splendid fall day!" said Mr. Biddle with delight.

He picked up his fishing pole and set off toward the path that led to the stream.

When he arrived at the water's edge, Mr. Biddle discovered one of his best friends, Alexander Tortoise, resting on the bank. He bent down over his hard, mottled shell and tapped twice.

"Are you awake?" asked Mr. Biddle in a low whisper.

Alexander raised his head and looked up at the bear.

"*G*ood day to you, Mr. Biddle," said Alexander in a small voice. *"What brings you down to the stream on this fine morning?"*

"A rather large appetite," said the bear, patting his vest-covered belly. *"Would you please tell me where I can catch a fish or two?"*

"It seems to me that the prospects are quite favorable over there," said Alexander, pointing toward a clump of hemlock trees.

"Well then," said Mr. Biddle. *"Let's have a look. Come along, little fellow."*

The friends were quiet for a time, as they traveled ever so slowly beside the murmuring stream. The edge of a brilliant sun was now gleaming through the trees, throwing spots of dancing light onto the water.

They reached the shady eaves of the rustling hemlocks.

Mr. Biddle looked around.

"Alexander, are you sure this is the proper place?" he asked. *"There's quite a smattering of spindly plants in the water."*

"Precisely," said Alexander. *"Fish enjoy drifting and flicking their tails amongst all sorts of bits and bobs."*

Mr. Biddle's expression changed from uncertainty to delight.

"Ah, yes, brilliant!"

So he stood under the canopy of trees and started to fish.

"Alexander, have I ever told you the tale of the two squirrels named Jonathan and Basil?"

"Indeed you have," said the tortoise. "Many, many times."

"Well, if you insist," said Mr. Biddle. "I will tell it to you one more time."

Alexander smiled. The bear cleared his throat importantly and began the familiar story…

In my youth, I was quite an independent cub. I explored this very riverside, always looking for new friends and adventures.

One afternoon, I came across Jonathan Squirrel. His long, bushy tail was grander than any I had ever seen. He was staring at the ground very intently.

"Hello, Jonathan," I said.

"Hello there, Mr. Biddle," said the squirrel, looking up briefly.

"What are you doing?" I asked curiously.

"I'm looking for my hickory nut," said Jonathan. "Would you like to help me find it?"

"Of course," I said kindly. "Now, which direction were you facing when you buried the nut? North or south?"

Jonathan peered left and right, frowning slightly.

"I believe it was somewhere between the two," he said, glancing at the gap between his legs.

"Hmmm," I said. *"That would put the nut in front of this big tree root."*

So we searched, there and everywhere.

"Did you find it?" Alexander asked.

He knew full well the answer to his question. This was, after all, the bear's favorite story.

"*Alas, we did not,*" said Mr. Biddle.

He pulled in the fishing line and tossed it back into the water.

"*Although, we did find Nigel Owl perched atop a large tree stump.*"

"*I don't like to spread bad news,*" said Nigel, blinking his lamp-like, amber eyes. "*But your valuable possession has been taken.*"

"*Who would take my cherished hickory nut?*" Jonathan asked, his heart sinking terribly.

"*Well…*" Nigel said, in a pompous tone. "*If you really want to know, and I assume that you do…*"

He paused for effect, slowly unfurling a wing and preening the feathers there with his pristine beak. "*I suggest,*" he said — perhaps even slower than before — extending his wing so that the tips of his speckled feathers caught a shaft of light and pointed to an area at the edge of the clearing, "*that you look for your answer over there.*"

Then, in the next moment, Nigel stretched his magnificent wings, thrust himself into the air, and soared silently into the horizon.

Jonathan turned on the spot and scampered to the very edge of the clearing. He patiently waited… sitting as still as a statue with his eyes fixed unblinkingly on a particularly dense patch of lavender-blue flowers. The woodland had never smelled so sweet.

Soon a small reddish-brown figure popped into view and scurried past him.

"Oho," Alexander muttered. *"I know this part — that was Basil Squirrel."*

"It was indeed. And he dashed away with Jonathan's hickory nut in hand." Mr. Biddle continued as if there had been no interruption.

"Jonathan's voice rang out, saying, "STOP, THIEF! COME BACK HERE THIS VERY INSTANT!"

A moment later, we pressed on through the forest.

Our pursuit led us farther into the depths of the woods. The minutes crept by. Then, we stopped abruptly, under a towering oak — close enough to hear Basil singing from high above:

"Frisky and clever am I,

Frisky and clever am I,

I can find a nut

Without batting an eye!"

Jonathan took a deep breath.

"Now, listen here, you silly squirrel," he said. *"I've had quite enough! That hickory nut is mine."*

"No, it's not," said Basil, springing from one tree to another. *"I found it, so I get to keep it."* With his next leap, a tree branch gave way, causing Basil to topple downward, falling face-first onto an enormous, mossy rock.

Basil felt as though his head was spinning very fast. He closed his eyes, wishing it would stop. A trickle of fear came over him.

"Someone, please, help me!" he called out desperately.

Without hesitation, we hurried to his side.

"You know," said Jonathan sharply. *"You would not be in this unfortunate situation if you hadn't taken my hickory nut in the first place."*

"Your hickory nut," said Basil, in a slightly disgruntled voice. *"I daresay we haven't made that determination yet."*

W e gently raised the feeble squirel onto his feet.

"Oh, thank you!" said Basil gratefully.

With one paw, he held the treasured hickory nut out to Jonathan and said, *"Please accept this as a token of my appreciation for your kind deed."*

"Thank you," said Jonathan. *"But before I enjoy eating this nut, I want to show you that it is mine. Do you see the carved letter on the front?"*

Basil examined the nut and nodded.

"Do you happen to know what the letter is?" Jonathan asked. A slight pause followed.

"I'm afraid that I do not," said Basil grimly.

"Why, what do you mean?" said Jonathan crisply. *"It's the letter J, and that stands for Jonathan."*

Basil lowered his head. *"I didn't know the nut was yours,"* he said, not looking either of us in the eye, *"because I've never been taught how to read or write."*

It suddenly occurred to Jonathan that Basil had not meant to steal his hickory nut at all

"**O**h, *Basil*," said Jonathan, no longer angry with the squirrel. *"There are so many important things to know in the world. How will you ever learn about them if you cannot read or write?"*

"I don't know," said Basil, timidly.

"**S**o, *what happened next?"* Alexander asked. Though he knew the bear's story well, each time he heard it was as intriguing as the first.

"Well..." said Mr. Biddle, his eyes fixed on the wind-ruffled surface of the water.

"What happened next is that, Jonathan made a very important decision — he forgave his friend and offered him a priceless gift."

"A gift?" Alexander asked. *"Do you mean the hickory nut?"*

"Not exactly," said Mr. Biddle. *"Jonathan would give him something incredibly more valuable than a hickory nut."*

The bear looked down at his friend, a knowing twinkle in his eye.

"Please, Mr. Biddle," said Alexander eagerly. *"Won't you finish the story? I want to hear what happens next."*

Mr. Biddle nodded and continued...

Basil stood silently in front of us, his eyes lingering over the ground.

Jonathan thought to himself for a minute, and then a wonderful idea occurred to him. *"Perhaps, we could teach you to read and write."*

"You would do that for me?" said Basil, with an air of great surprise.

"Absolutely," said Jonathan. *"But, only if you promise to cherish this gift and to always return the things you find to their rightful owners."*

"I promise," said Basil happily, flicking the end of his tail.

So, in the afternoons that followed, we gathered on this very riverbank and taught Basil Squirrel how to read and write. He was quite a good student.

Before winter's embrace, Basil had learned to engrave the letter B onto his own hickory nuts.

He was so grateful for Jonathan's kindness and generosity that he decided to give his new friend a special gift – his finest hickory nut, bearing the letter F for Friend.

Just then, the water rippled as a lovely brown trout began to bite at the fishing line. With one sharp tug, Mr. Biddle landed the fish and firmly pulled it towards the edge of the bank. The bear looked extremely pleased with himself.

"A perfect end to the day," said Mr. Biddle finally.

"To which story?" Alexander asked, yawning in the warm sunlight.

"Both, I suppose." Mr. Biddle said, unhooking the wriggling fish.

The tortoise wore a very kind smile and said, *"You know, I believe the tale gets better each time you tell it."*

Mr. Biddle was beaming. He turned to thank Alexander, but his friend had fallen fast asleep inside his cozy shell.

About the Author

As an explorer, entrepreneur, philanthropist, and author, Anne Mason's life reads like an extraordinary adventure book. Her journey began as a young girl traveling and studying throughout Europe — especially England — where she developed her love of teddy bears. As the years wore on, she took to exploring new heights — literally — as she scaled the frigid ascent to Mt. Everest's Base Camp (17,600 ft). From there she appeared as a principal actor in the 2009 adventure documentary film, *Journey to Everest,* wherein the American team narrowly escaped an icy fate after they were bumped from a flight at Lukla airport that would later crash in the mountains.

Back in the States, while recovering from a serious illness that suspended her traveling adventures, she took to exploring the confines of her own imagination. It was through this inward self-discovery that Mason first combined her passion for the teddy bear and her love of children to create the world of the delightfully wonderful "Mr. Biddle." Through a single teddy bear and his forest friends, Mason began her recovery, and built up a world that would allow others to experience the importance of friendship, adventure, learning and gratitude that she had learned throughout her own travels.

Mason invites you to join Mr. Biddle in Forest of Leeds to explore the bits and bobs that make up us all, and to experience the story you'll be retelling for years to come.

About the Photographer

Jim Zuckerman left his medical studies in 1970 to pursue his love of photography and turn it into a career. Jim specializes in wildlife, nature, and travel photography, macro work, photomicroscopy and digital effects. His diversity in technique and style is unique in the professional arena. He states that he only photographs beauty, leaving the dark side of life to other photographers. Jim is a contributing editor to *Petersen's Photographic Magazine* and *Shutterbug Magazine*, and he is the author of 25 books on photography.

His images, articles, and photo features have been published in scores of books and magazines including *Time-Life* books, publications of the *National Geographic Society, the Economist, Omi Magazine,* and *Life Magazine*. He now teaches many online photo courses for Betterphoto.com. Jim also leads photography tours to exotic destinations such as Indonesia, Turkey, Namibia, Kenya, Kazakhstan, Patagonia, and Mongolia.

Made in the USA
Columbia, SC
25 October 2017